This edition first published in 2017 by Gecko Press

PO Box 9335, Marion Square,
Wellington 6141, New Zealand

info@geckopress.com

English language edition © Gecko Press Ltd 2017
Translation © Sally-Ann Spencer 2017
Text and illustrations © Antje Damm 2016

Title of the original edition *Warten auf Goliath*
© 2016 Moritz Verlag, Frankfurt am Main
English-language edition arranged through
Mundt Agency, Düsseldorf

Distributed in the United States and Canada by
Lerner Publishing Group, www.lernerbooks.com

Distributed in the United Kingdom by Bounce Sales
and Marketing, www.bouncemarketing.co.uk

Distributed in Australia by Scholastic Australia,
www.scholastic.com.au

Distributed in New Zealand by Upstart Distribution,
www.upstartpress.co.nz

Edited by Penelope Todd
Design and typesetting by Spencer Levine

Printed in China by Everbest Printing Co Ltd,
an accredited ISO 14001 & FSC certified printer

ISBN hardback: 978-1-776571-41-3
ISBN paperback: 978-1-776571-42-0

For more curiously good books
visit www.geckopress.com

Waiting for Goliath

Antje Damm

GECKO PRESS

Bear has been
sitting and waiting
since dawn.

"I'm waiting for Goliath,"
he tells everyone.
"Goliath is coming!
He's my best friend."

"Is he as strong as you?" asks Robin.
"Much stronger," says Bear.
"And smart! He can count to eighteen!"

Bear dozes off. He snores and dreams and waits for Goliath.

"Your Goliath isn't coming," says Robin.
"Of course he is!" says Bear.
"He is definitely coming. You'll see."

Bear goes behind a bush.
The robins twitter.
"Quick, Bear,
someone's here!"

"Is he behaving himself?
Does he smell nice?" asks Bear.
"Not exactly," say the robins.
"Then it's not Goliath!" growls Bear.

A bus pulls up and the doors open...

But no one gets out.

The birds have flown
away for winter.

Sometimes Bear forgets
that he is waiting for Goliath.

He feels sleepier and sleepier.

When he wakes up,
it is warm again.

He hears a faint noise like a hand sliding slowly across paper. Goliath is coming!

"Goliath!" says Bear. "You made it!"

"I'm sorry," says Goliath. "I came as fast as I could."

"Never mind," says Bear. "You're here now."

"And I know exactly what
we're going to do!"